The Lonely Mare

By Doug Gaither

PublishAmerica
Baltimore

First printing

ISBN: 978-1-4489-5871-9
PUBLISHED BY PUBLISHAMERICA, LLLP
www.publishamerica.com
Baltimore

Printed in the United States of America

In a grassy yard lived a lonely little mare. Each day she had only a fence at to stare.

Butterscotch, the small blonde horse, only wanted a friend to play with, of course.

On Monday she was lonely,
On Tuesday she was lonely,
On Wednesday she was lonely,
And on Thursday, guess what? She was lonely

1

The fence was a jail for this small mare and kept out the dream of finding a friend somewhere.

On Friday she was lonely,
On Saturday she was lonely
And on Sunday, guess what? She was lonely.

3

"What is this?" "What noise do I hear?" Said the tiny horse, "Should I be full of fear?"

The horse stretched her neck as far as she could to see over the fence made of thick rough wood.

On Monday she was afraid,
On Tuesday she was afraid,
On Wednesday she was afraid,
And on Thursday, guess what? She was afraid.

5

Her fear grew stronger as she thought in fright, should I run and hide with all my might?

On Friday she was afraid,
On Saturday she was afraid,
And on Sunday, guess what? She was afraid.

What were these over the tall wooden jail? --Two small black bundles with two small black tails.

The gate flew open and in quickly scurried two little dark creatures, playful and hurried.

On Monday she was curious,
On Tuesday she was curious,
On Wednesday she was curious,
And on Thursday, guess what? She was curious.

Could her dream come true with these two goats? Could she now have friends with furry black coats?

On Friday she was curious,
On Saturday she was curious,
And on Sunday, guess what? She was curious.

I'll name one Spit and I'll name one Spot," said the tiny mare who loved them a lot.

The three new buddies played all day—chasing tails, butting heads, and eating fresh hay.

On Monday they played,
On Tuesday they played,
On Wednesday they played,
And on Thursday, guess what? They played.

Her friends filled each day with joy so rare, she thought to herself this little blonde mare.

On Friday they played,
On Saturday they played,
And on Sunday, guess what? They played.

She had no memory of lonely days, before Spit and Spot came forever to stay.

Who could imagine a friendship so dear would grow and blossom in just one year.

Through Monday to Wednesday, they were happy,
Through Thursday to Sunday, they were happy,
And each day of the week for the rest of their lives, guess what?
They were happy.

17